E   38200
Tra   Trapani, Iza.

        Haunted party.

HAUNTED PARTY

Iza Trapani

NJ-SP Elementary
North Judson, Indiana
 Charlesbridge
38200

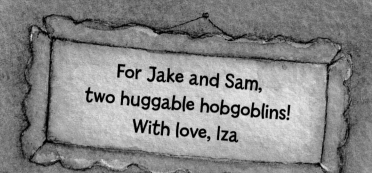

For Jake and Sam,
two huggable hobgoblins!
With love, Iza

2010 First paperback edition
Copyright © 2009 by Iza Trapani

Published by Charlesbridge
85 Main Street
Watertown, MA 02472
(617) 926-0329
www.charlesbridge.com

Library of Congress Cataloging-in-Publication Data
Trapani, Iza.
    Haunted Party / Iza Trapani.
        p. cm.
    Summary: In this counting book that introduces the numbers from one
to ten, a ghost and his supernatural friends have a party on Halloween night.
    ISBN 978-1-58089-246-9 (reinforced for library use)
    ISBN 978-1-58089-247-6 (softcover)
[1. Stories in rhyme. 2. Halloween—Fiction. 3. Parties—Fiction.
4. Supernatural—Fiction. 5. Haunted houses—Fiction. 6. Counting.] I. Title.
PZ8.3.T686Hau 2009
[E]—dc22   2008025330

 in China
8 7 6 5 4 3 2
7 6 5 4 3 2 1

 in watercolor, colored pencil, and ink
 s paper (cold press)
 type set in Ghost Show and Billy
 ma Graphics, Singapore
 y 2010 in Nansha, Guangdong, China
 mpany, Ltd. through Four Colour
 entucky
 n G. Walker

It's Halloween and what a night!
The full moon shines. The bats take flight.
Here at this haunted house **1** ghost
Has been a very busy host,
Preparing for a ton of fun.
At last the party has begun!
The doorbell chimes some eerie notes,
And to the door the ghost host floats.

2 spooky skeletons come in,
With rattly bones and toothy grins,
To boogie as the record spins
At the haunted house of the ghost.

3 gruesome goblins, gross and green,
With pointy ears that aren't too clean,
Enjoy some really mean cuisine
At the haunted house of the ghost.

4 wild werewolves, very hairy,
5 vile vampires, super scary,
Are apple bobbers extraordinary
At the haunted house of the ghost.

6 ghastly ghouls, who glare and gaze
With creepy, sunken eyes ablaze,
Are in a pumpkin-carving craze
At the haunted house of the ghost.

7 mean monsters, crass and crude,
Such party poopers acting rude,
Are in a pumpkin-smashing mood
At the haunted house of the ghost.

8 wretched witches, riding on brooms,
9 morbid mummies, risen from tombs,
Kick up their heels in the dreadful rooms
At the haunted house of the ghost.

10 cute children, sunny and sweet,
With smiling faces come to greet,
Politely chanting, "Trick or Treat!"
At the haunted house of the ghost.

9 morbid mummies flee and hide.

8 wretched witches zoom outside.

7 mean monsters tremble with fear.

6 ghastly ghouls try to disappear.

5 vile vampires soar in flight.

4 wild werewolves howl in fright.

3 gruesome goblins quake and quiver.
2 spooky skeletons shake and shiver.

But who of them was frightened most?

Not the ghost!